THE GUNNYWOLF

RETOLD AND ILLUSTRATED BY A. DELANEY

HarperTrophy
A Division of HarperCollinsPublishers

I'd like to thank the many people who so generously and earnestly and enthusiastically helped me find other tellings of *The Gunnywolf*. I am indebted to the New York Public Library system, with its magnificent resources and facilities, and to the very able people who work there. I'd particularly like to thank the anonymous woman in the Telephone Reference Service of the New York Public Library who helped me so by telling me where to look for early versions of *The Gunnywolf*. Thank you to her coworkers in the Telephone Reference Service, to the librarians in the Central Children's Room of the Donnell Library Center of the New York Public Library, and to the librarians of the Cooperative Services Division of the New York Public Library. The New York Public Library enabled me to use Butler Library at Columbia University; thank you to the librarians there.

Mrs. Laurie Bready, Sawyer Free Library, Gloucester, Massachusetts, was very helpful to me, as were Mrs. Alfreda Irwin, Chautauqua Institution, Chautauqua, New York; Dr. Robert A. McCown, Special Collections and Manuscripts Library, The University of Iowa, Iowa City, Iowa; and Mrs. Sonia L. Jacobs, Special Collections Department, Rare Books Room, University of Colorado at Boulder, Colorado; I'm grateful to them. Thank you to Mr. Charles Camp, American Folklore Society, Baltimore, Maryland; and to Dr. Linda Degh, Folklore Institute, Indiana University, Bloomington, Indiana. And thank you to Mr. John Delaney, FIND/SVP, New York.

Editors are nice too; many warm thanks to Nina Ignatowicz and Pam Hastings for their faith in *The Gunnywolf*, and for their patience with me.

Library of Congress Cataloging-in-Publication Data
Delaney, A.
    The gunnywolf / retold and illustrated by A. Delaney.—1st ed.
        p.   cm.
    Summary: A little girl wanders into the woods to pick flowers and meets the dreaded Gunnywolf.
    ISBN 0-06-021594-1
    ISBN 0-06-021595-X (lib. bdg.)
    [1. Wolves—Folklore.   2. Alphabet—Folklore.   3. Folklore.]   I. Title.
PZ8.1.D379Gu 1988   87-29351
398.2′452974442—dc19   CIP
[E]   AC

A Scott Foresman Edition
ISBN 0-673-80093-8

To David

Once upon a time, a Little Girl and her father
lived next to a deep, dark woods.

The Little Girl never went into the woods.

Nobody did. The Gunnywolf lived there.

But one day, the Little Girl saw
a flower blooming just inside the woods.

The Little Girl forgot all about the Gunnywolf.
She stepped between the trees
and picked the flower.
And she sang,
"A B C D E F G
H I J K L M N O P
Q R S T U V
W X Y Z."

When the Little Girl looked up, she saw more flowers.
Again she forgot about the Gunnywolf.

The Little Girl skipped deeper into the woods and picked the flowers.
And she sang,
"A B C D E F G H I J K L M N O P Q R S T U V—"

When th... she saw e...

Who are the characters in the story?

Again she forgot about the Gunnywolf.

The Little Girl ran deep into the woods and picked the flowers.
And she sang,
"A B C D E F G
H I J K L M N O P—"

The Little Girl was far from home.
Holding her flowers, she turned to go, and—

THERE WAS THE GUNNYWOLF!

"Little Girl!" said the Gunnywolf.
"Sing that good, sweet song to me."

"abcdefghijklmnopqrstuvwxyz," sang the Little Girl
in a tiny voice.

"M
   M
      N
         A
            B,"
sang the Gunnywolf,
and he fell sound asleep.

The Little Girl ran away as fast as she could.
Pit-a-pat, pit-a-pat, pit-a-pat, pit-a-pat!

The Gunnywolf woke up!

Un-ka-cha! Un-ka-cha! Un-ka-cha! Un-ka-cha!
He ran, and soon he caught up with the Little Girl.

"Little girl!" said the Gunnywolf.
"Sing that good, sweet song again."

"A B C D E F G H I J K L M N O P Q R S T U V W X Y Z,"
sang the Little Girl.

"Q
  R
    L
     S
      P,"
sang the Gunnywolf,
and he fell sound asleep.

Pit-a-pat, pit-a-pat, pit-a-pat, pit-a-pat!

The Little Girl ran back through the woods as fast as she could.

The Gunnywolf woke up!
Un-ka-cha! Un-ka-cha! Un-ka-cha! Un-ka-cha!
He ran, and again he caught up with the Little Girl.

"Little Girl!" said the Gunnywolf.
"Sing that good, sweet song again."

"A B C D E F G H I J K L M N O P Q R S T U V W X Y Z,"
sang the Little Girl.

"X
  Y
    Z
      Z
        z,"
sang the Gunnywolf,
and he fell sound asleep.

Pit-a-pat, pit-a-pat, pit-a-pat, pit-a-pat!

KEEP OUT

The Little Girl ran out of the woods.

"Whew!" said the Little Girl.

But the next day and every day after that, when the Little Girl went outside,

she gathered flowers and more flowers and even more flowers.

And she sang,
"A B C D E F G
H I J K L M N O P
Q R S T U V
W X Y Z."